BY THE SAME AUTHOR

Mr. Upstairs and Mr. Downstairs

The Crumb That Walked

Hunch, Munch

Hunch, Munch and Crunch

and Crunch

More about the Jonquils

BY CHARLES NORMAN

PICTURES BY *Margaret Bloy Graham*

HARPER & BROTHERS, PUBLISHERS

G

Library of Congress catalog card number: 51-13012

To

Kathy and Timmy
Bobby, too,
Win and Jimmy
Karen Sue,
Samuel Adams
and
Christina,
Francine
Fredi
and
Edwina,
Lucy
Katie
Sheila
Gail,
Cynthia, small,
Margaret, tall,
Biddy
Pammy
Tony
Paul,
Jane
Parkman
Charles
AND
Jane Jonquil

CONTENTS

Preface for Parents   1

The Cowboys and Indians of New York   5

A Rendezvous in Central Park   9

The Woman in the Corkscrew Hat   15

The Animals in the Zoo   20

Hunch, Munch and Crunch   25

The Life and Happy Times of Mrs. Jonquil   32

The Life and Happy Times of Mrs. Jonquil (Continued)   35

Mr. Jonquil's Fairy Tale   38

Mr. Jonquil's Fairy Tale (Concluded by Mrs. Jonquil)   41

The Life and Happy Times of Mrs. Jonquil (Concluded)   43

Hunch, Munch and Crunch

Preface for Parents

LOOKING BACK, Mr. Jonquil could see that his life was divided into two periods: the years of self-centered youth before he became a father, and the time dating from a winter day when he saw a baby with blue eyes gazing up at him from a hospital basket and a tiny hand reached out and grasped his heart, never to let go.

He knew, of course, that his intellectual friends would say, cynically smiling, that a baby's eyes are not coordinated sufficiently half an hour after birth to look up at him exactly the way he would have described it, but they might just as well tell him that a tiny hand grasping his heart was only a figure of speech.

"No, no," he would have said; "I am only trying to relate how another young man with thoroughly selfish instincts experienced the greatest adventure of his life, and of his humility before a new kind of love that asked for nothing as a seal or sign."

Up to the age of twenty-five, when the adventure befell him, he had managed to retain—it was no great struggle—an astonishing interest in himself and his affairs. Children had never attracted him; on the contrary, the din they make in the world had always distressed him.

1

Then, one day, he learned that Mrs. Jonquil was going to have a baby. She was not knitting a tiny pink sweater—indeed, he did not recall that she ever began one. In view of what happened, it was not necessary for her to have done so. There was also an absence of everything that novelists describe and moving pictures copy, with soft music.

He was pleased, of course, and a little proud; nevertheless, he was at once beset by doubts and fears. "Lord," he thought, "the things we are taught at home and in school, but never anything that might be useful the two or three times in life when we discover our ignorance and helplessness!"

He appealed to a scientifically-minded friend, a veteran married man compared with him, and was comforted by his words, backed up by a book from the shelf. The odds were long against a mischance. How superior his friend seemed, how detached. He had no children.

Then a new anxiety appeared. Would it be a boy or a girl? Mr. Jonquil hoped for a boy.

Meanwhile, he and Mrs. Jonquil moved in a realm of expectancy, a realm lapped daily by wool wavelets from relatives and friends.

Many times it appeared as though the great event was at hand— once or twice practically upon them. When, finally, they took a taxi to the hospital, it was calmly enough. Mr. Jonquil did not fail to notice that the role of Mrs. Jonquil's mother was more important, perhaps even more respectable, than his.

He waited.

"It's a girl," he was told at last by a smiling, superior nurse, and was led into a room whose chief adornment was a wicker basket overflowing with blanket.

Mr. Jonquil saw there, beneath him, a pink, round face starred by two blue eyes that looked at him hard and long. "O my literal-minded friends, I swear it!" he would have told them. Two little red feet squirmed happily, and a tiny red fist rose from the ripples of blanket.

Mr. Jonquil also gazed hard and long; if she had been Helen of

Troy, he could not have been more fascinated by her strange, dear beauty, or more completely under her domination. For, standing there, he found himself vowing that this child, this stranger whom he had known but an instant, would never lack because of any failure in him; that thenceforward he was her servant, her slave; and he was glad to be able to make that vow.

Then the nurse came back and lifted his new love to his shoulder, and his arm went around her. He never again thought of a boy-child.

All at once, the world that had been peopled merely by men and women became transformed. Men and women never seem to see each other until they are introduced; but children always recognize each other, with a look that says:

"How do you do?
Who are you?
I am I,
By the by."

Out of the din that children make the children stood forth, and he saw them for the first time—the individual, secret and subtle beings of extraordinary perceptions, extraordinary gifts, occasionally wide-eyed or bewildered over adult fumbling and fury. Mr. Jonquil found himself on the side of the children. Against the world of adults even the mean and mischievous ones were his wards, for they had reasons (these things, of course, he learned in time).

But that winter day in the street, every time he passed a child in a carriage, he wanted to take it into his arms for the sake of a certain child swaddled in a hospital blanket. He smiled at parents and all the children he saw. He became the self-appointed guardian of children bullied by those older than themselves; and occasionally, since then, he has told one or two parents what he thought of them for knocking their offspring on the head with the flat of a handbag or clouting them over the ear with a sharp palm.

The Cowboys and Indians
of New York

IT WAS story-telling time in the Jonquil house.

A wisp of a moon hung like wash above the yard.

Stars sprouted like glass flowers on the upside-down lawn of the sky.

Jane Jonquil was in bed. Her father sat beside the bed. But before he could begin a story, Jane suddenly asked: "Where did you grow up?"

"In New York City," said Mr. Jonquil.

"What did you do?" asked Jane.

"I played games," said Mr. Jonquil, "like all the other little people who live close to the sidewalk."

"What little people?" asked Jane, who was not so big.

"Children," said Mr. Jonquil, who was no longer little.

"What kind of games?" asked Jane, and settled herself comfortably.

"Cops and robbers," said Mr. Jonquil. "Bang, bang— you're dead—I'm not—yes, you are—no, I'm not, you missed me—you are, too. Everybody wanted to be cops, because the robbers were always being shot dead or captured alive and handcuffed, which was humiliating. So we played cowboys and Indians mostly, because nobody minded being an Indian, and I need hardly say nobody minded being a cowboy.

5

"Our rifles were made out of slats, our bows and arrows from the ribs of old umbrellas. *Bang!* went my trusty rifle, and another redskin bit the dust, or was supposed to, but sometimes he just slunk off and jeered: 'Yah, yah, you missed me.' Then he would twang his bow, and an arrow whizzed over my head. I'd fire again from behind a lamp-post or stoop. No luck.

" 'Sheriff,' I'd say, 'that's an ornery crittur out there, seems like no bullet made by human hands can stop him.'

" 'Pardner,' said the sheriff, 'I reckon you said a mouthful.'

" 'Well, sir,' I'd say to the sheriff—he was a fat boy from down the block a piece—'let's capture him alive.'

" 'And tie him up good and proper,' said the sheriff, his eyes sparkling. 'Then we can torture him and get the secret of the gold mine out of him.'

"So then the sheriff galloped off, making believe he was galloping home, while I just stayed there, drawing another bead on the redskin varmint. Suddenly the sheriff veers about on his pinto pony, and before you could say *Buffalo Bill!* he pounces on the crittur with a whoop. The redskin lets out a yell you could hear in the next block. That brings me on the gallop, too, with my trusty lasso, and we tie him up, arms and feet, legs and hands, like a mummy.

"Then up goes a window right over our heads, and out pops his mother's head in curlers. The sheriff looks up and so do I.

6

" 'Pardner,' he says to me, 'the Indians are on the warpath; I see them a-headin' and a-comin' right this way, with war paint on.'

" 'Sheriff,' I said, 'I reckon that was a right proper mouthful, too. As for you,' I said to our captive, 'I'll settle with you later.' "

"Did you?" asked Jane.

"Yes," said her father. "The next day I traded a hatful of marbles to get my lasso back.

"And that," he concluded, "was the way we played cowboys and Indians in the streets of New York."

A Rendezvous in Central Park

"WHAT ELSE did you do when you were little?" Jane asked her father.

"I went exploring in Central Park," said Mr. Jonquil. "Central Park is very big. It is in New York City, which is not little. There are eight million people in New York City. One, two, three, four, five, six, seven, eight. Add six zeros, and you have 8,000,000.

"There are probably a few hundred thousand extra or additional supernumerary but not superfluous men and women, girls and boys, in those round zeros. Not to mention several hundred thousand cats and dogs. And the birds in the park. And birds in cages. And the animals in the Zoo.

"The biggest animals, of course, are the elephants.

9

The elephants are big,
But I don't know why;
Then come the
Hippopotami.

That's the plural of
Hippopotamus,
Not to be confused
With the platypus.

The platypus is small,
But has a big snout
For shoveling things in
That he finds out.

On the other hand,
The hippopotami
Have plenty of hip
And a poached-egg eye,
And are very low
Where the elephants are high.

"The tallest animal is the giraffe. A word of advice about
the giraffe:

It isn't nice
For us to laugh
At the lean, long,
Lank giraffe.

Of course, he's thin
And very tall,
And his neck is the longest
Neck of all.

But he's made that way
To nibble at ease,
With his neck 'way up
In the mulberry trees.

So there's really no reason
For us to laugh
At the lean, long,
Lank giraffe.

"The smallest animals are the squirrels; but these, of course, are not in cages. They're as free as the birds, some of which are very strange and don't even sound like birds. Take

THE CASSOWARY

The cassowary is a bird;
It's like an ostrich, I have heard;
If you could ever catch it whole,
It would go in a casserole,
A cassowary casserole.
Unfortunately for this plan,
It runs far faster than a man;
In fact, it may turn out to be

Hunch, Munch and Crunch

A little difficult to see.
Therefore my best advice is this
(I give it in parenthesis)
While hunting for a cassowary
The safest thing would be to carry

A Rendezvous in Central Park

A sandwich that's already made
Which you can gobble in the shade.
It's different with the cassowary;
No other bird is so contrary;
It doesn't mind about the sun,
So long as it can run and run,
And have a little simple fun.

"So much for the cassowary," concluded Mr. Jonquil.

"You haven't said anything about exploring yet," Jane reminded him.

"In the summertime," said Mr. Jonquil, "my friends and I rowed across the lake in Central Park. By the time we got

to the other side we were pirates. We would beach the boat where no one could find it, and go exploring for a cave—a nice dank and dark sort of cave, of course. We carried a little wooden box with us for a table, and stuck a candle on it, and swore eternal friendship by its light."

"And then?" asked Jane.

"And then," said Mr. Jonquil in a low voice, "we plotted horrible deeds."

"Did you ever do them?" demanded Jane hopefully.

"It's not so easy to do horrible deeds, even with practice, if you have been brought up right," Mr. Jonquil said apologetically. "So along about the time that they were to be done, the boat had to be taken back, or we got frightfully hungry; and while no one wished to admit it, it did seem wiser to start back instead of staying any longer in that dark, dank cave with the candle burning low."

"Will you take me to Central Park?" asked Jane.

"Tomorrow," said her father, and Jane fell asleep.

The Woman in the Corkscrew Hat

THE NEXT day was Sunday.

Jane Jonquil and her father walked to Washington Square to get a bus uptown.

On one corner there was a garage. It had a sign which said:

WE FIX FLATS.

On the opposite corner was a clothing store. It had a sign which read:

WE FIT FATS.

15

On a brick wall, in chalk, was written: *"Beverly loves and will marry two men."*

Jane Jonquil and her father got on a bus. As they rode up Fifth Avenue, the manikins in the shop windows watched them go by. The manikins were elegantly dressed, but they weren't going anywhere. They just stood, elegant and serene, behind cool plate glass. The bus swished uptown between two corridors of serene figures in the shop windows of Fifth Avenue.

Then Jane saw the park stretching out its branches over the sidewalk, and Mr. Jonquil knew they had only a few more blocks to go.

As soon as the bus came opposite the Zoo, Jane and her father got out and crossed Fifth Avenue. All around them men and women promenaded. On other streets they merely walk; but on Fifth Avenue they promenade. A woman promenaded past them with her nose in the air and a poodle on a leash.

"What is that on top of her head?" whispered Mr. Jonquil.

"A hat, of course," said Jane.

The hat of the woman with the poodle on a leash did not surprise Jane, because she was a female; but it surprised Mr. Jonquil, who was not.

"I'm dizzy," he said; "let's sit down."

They sat down on a bench outside the park, and Mr. Jonquil remarked:

"Do you see that woman in the corkscrew hat?
She didn't say;
I didn't know;
Neither of us knew;
Where she,
I or we,
Were at,
Because of that corkscrew hat."

Then Jane and her father got up from the bench and went into the park. They went down the steps that led to the Zoo and straight to the balloon man blowing up balloons with helium instead of air, because helium is a gas and more floaty. He would take a flat, flabby balloon from a pile of flat, flabby balloons and put its snout to the spout of the helium tank, and *whish! swish!* the balloon became fat, tight and full, and shivered ecstatically when the balloon man gave it a bump, thump, and also a bounce, jounce.

As soon as the balloon man saw Jane he took a red balloon from a pile of flabby balloons and put its snout to the spout on the helium tank. Instantly the red balloon filled out: *whish! swish!* And as soon as the balloon was full, you could see "Central Park Zoo" stamped on one side of it in big letters, and on the other side a bear.

Then Mr. Jonquil paid the balloon man and he and Jane walked away, with the balloon sailing along by a string and all full of itself, very thumpy, bumpy, and bouncy, jouncy. They stopped to buy a bag of peanuts, which Mr. Jonquil put in his pocket; and when Jane looked back, she saw the balloon man looking at her. His face was all mustache and a smile.

The Animals in the Zoo

"IS THIS where you came when you were little?" Jane Jonquil asked her father.

"Yes," said Mr. Jonquil. "The very spot."

He was holding Jane's free hand, and she gave his a squeeze.

From her other hand sprouted the red balloon.

The red balloon walked stiffly on its string above Jane's wrist. It floated past the elephants standing like iron monuments behind their iron fence. They didn't even flap their ears or curl their trunks. They just stood and stared. How anything so big could do so little is a mystery.

The balloon went past the hippopotami wallowing in their muddy pool.

The Animals in the Zoo

The muddy hippopotami
Were very low where the elephants were high;
They sagged in the middle where they were wide,
And dozed in the water side by side,
The hippy, happy hippopotami.

      The shaggy yak
      Showed his back.

The kneeling camels chewed like cows;
The macaws ca-cawed under the boughs.

The slinky fox paced back and forth,
And wished he were a hundred miles north,
Free to hunt for weasels and chicks;
He dreamed of catching five or six
For breakfast, or maybe afternoon tea,
Or a little snack between two and three.

The whiskered seals looked moist and cool
As they slithered in and out of their pool.

      But the polar bear
      Didn't care
      Who stopped to stare;
      He slept with his paws
      Up in the air.

The lion padded to and fro;
The tiger had no place to go;
The leopard looked like a tabby cat,
But the habits and the habitat
Of the leopard are very different from
The habits and the habitat
Of the blinky, slinky tabby cat.

The balloon rode proudly above Jane's wrist right into the monkey house, where

A big baboon
With a snout for a nose,
Hairy fingers,
And hairy toes,
Hung,
Clung,
And swung,
Inside a cage
Which had a sign with his name and age.
He scratched his chest,
And also his head,
Which shows that he was
Rather ill-bred;
"But what can you
Expect to do
With a baboon?"

Jane said to the bear on her balloon.

Hunch, Munch and Crunch

IN THIS manner, Jane and her father saw all the animals in the Zoo. When they came out of the monkey house, Jane pointed to a long, low building with a terrace in front and round green tables on the terrace and people sitting around the tables.

"Are they eating?" she asked hopefully.

"Yes," said Mr. Jonquil.

It was the Zoo cafeteria.

"I'm hungry," said Jane.

"I move we eat," said her father.

"Second the motion," said Jane.

So they went into the cafeteria, the balloon with "Central Park Zoo" on it riding above Jane's wrist. Inside they saw a long counter with white-aproned men behind it, and on this counter all kinds of things to eat jumbled together and side

25

by side: pickles and pudding, ice cream and mustard, soup and sop, and bottles of pop, and

PLEASE KEEP MOVING

and

DO NOT STOP,

said signs behind the counter.

"Would you rather eat here or have a picnic?" asked Mr. Jonquil.

"A picnic," said Jane.

"Very well," said her father. "Would you like a picnic chicken sandwich?"

"Yes," said Jane, who was hungry enough to eat a hippopotamus.

"Two chicken sandwiches to take out," said Mr. Jonquil.

"Two chickens to go," said the man behind the counter.

Then Jane and her father moved along and came to the desserts. There was chocolate pudding, and banana cream pie; rice pudding, and cherry pie; tapioca pudding, and apple pie.

> Pie and pudding,
> Pudding and pie,

Jane and her father
  Passed them by.

They passed them by
  Because they were
Too squashy for
  A picnicker.

And chose instead
  A pile of plain
Cookies wrapped
  In cellophane.

"Two milks to go," said Mr. Jonquil. Two containers of milk appeared. They now had enough for an outdoors snack-eroo. Mr. Jonquil paid the cashier, and then he and Jane were off to their picnic in the park, with the red balloon riding stiff on its string above Jane's wrist.

Past the Zoo, in the interior of the park, little hills rise. There, rocks and trees and birds and squirrels are more plentiful than people. On one of these hills, under some trees, Jane and her father sat down and spread paper napkins in their laps.

"Did you explore here when you were little?" Jane asked.

"Yes," said Mr. Jonquil, gazing around him at the scenes of his childhood.

This seemed to please Jane, and the balloon bobbed up and down above her wrist as she began to eat.

No sooner had the picnic begun, however, than upside down from a tree came a squirrel and stared at them. His eyes were like shoe buttons with a high polish. His stare seemed to say:

"Here is a nice-looking man, probably with one of those funny names that people have; and a little girl, probably with one of those nice names little girls usually get; and both of them have food, and I'm sure they won't want to keep everything for themselves, and even if they do, some crumbs are sure to drop down, for I never yet saw a little girl—or boy, for that matter—who didn't drop crumbs while eating. So I think I'll just stay here."

That was the squirrel's first thought. His second one was: "Quite a few of these long-legged creatures carry peanuts around with them. It is just possible that these two have some, though they don't seem to be anywhere in sight. Naturally, I don't want their old sandwiches if I can have peanuts."

Jane saw the squirrel first. She nudged her father. Mr. Jonquil looked. He put the sandwich on the napkin in his lap and reached into his pocket. Out came the bag of peanuts. He poured some of the peanuts into Jane's hand, and she threw several at the squirrel. But before you could say "hist-whist," the squirrel was gone. When he got to the top of the tree, he looked down, and saw the peanuts lying on the ground. So before you could say "whist-hist," he was down again and hunched over a peanut in his paws, his tail curled upward and doing a kind of furry dance to and fro and back and forth.

29

The squirrel didn't know it, but another pair of squirrel eyes, bright as shoe buttons, were on him; for the next moment, out whisked Number Two, and snatched up a peanut, and shelled it quicker than you could think of saying anything, and was munching away. Number One looked at Number Two and thought: "An interloper!" He hunched his shoulders some more over the peanut he was nibbling.

Jane threw some more peanuts, and a third squirrel appeared. He was thinner than the first two, and his tail was sparsely covered with fur. But his eyes were just as bright, and when it came to picking up a peanut and crunching away, he was just as quick.

"Hunch, Munch and Crunch," said Jane, christening the three of them.

She threw the last of the peanuts at their feet, and while Hunch, Munch and Crunch gorged themselves, she and her father finished their sandwiches and drank their milk out of the containers, and watched. Jane, of course, still had her cookies, but these were for the journey home.

The Life and Happy Times

of Mrs. Jonquil

"WHERE did you live when you were little?" Jane asked her mother that night.

"On a farm in Iowa," said Mrs. Jonquil.

"What did you do?" Jane persisted.

"Lots of things," said her mother. She was trying to remember them all. Her memory was like a silent motion picture unwinding the past.

"The Life and Happy Times of Mrs. Jonquil as a girl," said Mr. Jonquil as though reading her thoughts. "In two reels. SCENE ONE: A FARM. Enter Miss Pomfret on a palfrey."

"Who?" asked Jane.

"Your mother, my dear, before I married her," said Mr. Jonquil. "Her name was Pomfret."

"What's a palfrey?" asked Jane.

"A horse for ladies," said Mr. Jonquil.

"What is it really—a palfrey?" Jane asked her mother.

"It was a plow horse," said Mrs. Jonquil. "But to me it was a palfrey. I had an old felt hat with a big feather stuck in it, and a wooden sword, and I rode around like a knight of old."

"A female knight," said Mr. Jonquil.

"What else did you do?" asked Jane.

"SCENE TWO of the life and happy times of Mrs. Jonquil," said Mr. Jonquil.

"I went on hay rides and sleigh rides," said Mrs. Jonquil. "And I picked berries in the woods and squeezed the juice out of them and made drinks with sugar and water. Then I sold the drinks for a penny a glass.

"Faugh," exclaimed Mrs. Jonquil, suddenly remembering the taste; "the drinks were awful, but the grownups bought them and even drank them down, and it didn't seem to do them any harm.

"With the pennies I got, I went to the store to buy candy, all kinds and shapes and colors—licorice drops, gum drops, jelly beans and marshmallow kewpies. The candy you could buy in those days for a penny! Why, the storekeeper had a scoop just for scooping up candy, and he would scoop up enough to fill a paper bag. Then he would give the bag a twist at the top, so the candy wouldn't spill out, and hand it over the counter very politely. Everybody was polite in those days."

"Aren't you asleep yet?" Mr. Jonquil asked Jane.

"Of course not," said Jane. "It wouldn't be polite."

The Life and Happy Times
of Mrs. Jonquil (Continued)

IT WAS story-telling time again in the Jonquil house.

"The happy girlhood of Miss Pomfret, now Mrs. Jonquil," said Mr. Jonquil.

Jane settled herself comfortably on the pillow.

"I had paper dolls, all of them named for actresses," said Mrs. Jonquil. "My favorite doll and leading lady was Irene Castle, a beautiful dancer. My next-to-the-favorite doll was Pearl White, a moving picture heroine."

"I know someone named White," said Jane.

"Who?" asked her mother.

"It's a secret," said Jane.

"Very well," said her mother. "I also had a teddy-bear named Mr. Moe. In fact, I had him in an old trunk until about a year ago. I wonder what became of him."

Before she could go on, Jane had thrown the cover back and leaped out of bed. To the astonishment of her mother and father she ran to the closet, reached in, and then ran back, clutching in her hands a battered teddy-bear.

"Is this it?" asked Jane when she was once more in bed.

"Well," said Mrs. Jonquil, "it's the right size."

"It's Mr. Moe," said Jane. "Only his name isn't Mr. Moe any more. It's T. White."

"Why 'T. White'?" asked Mrs. Jonquil.

" 'T' is for teddy," Jane explained, "and 'White' is for his hair. Only he hasn't got hair any more. He's white all over."

"He certainly has aged," said Mrs. Jonquil.

He certainly had. Over his chest he wore a tight little striped T-shirt to cover the stitches of an operation he had had, and while he could still sit up, he could no longer stand. But his nose was as sharp and wistful as ever it was when sniffing the delectable aromas of the past, and his shoe-button eyes had lost none of their eager brightness.

"I'm glad he's still in the family," said Mrs. Jonquil.

"SOFT MUSIC," said Mr. Jonquil.

"Next scene," said Jane.

"Very well," said Mrs. Jonquil. "We played hide-and-seek

36

outside the house, just as dusk was falling. Everything was weird, the trees melted like water, and the dark places got darker and darker.

"Oh, how we scared the dickens out of each other, jumping on somebody in the dark, or—worse—getting jumped on. I can feel the sensation even now.

"And when it was too dark to play, we sang together, and the stars came out, and a moon sailed along very fast. Sometimes grandfather came, and I sat on his knee while he skinned sugar cane and gave me a piece to suck, and he would tell me stories or read one to me and Mr. Moe when we got into bed."

"What kind of stories?" asked Jane.

"Fairy tales," said Mrs. Jonquil.

"Tell me one," said Jane, and settled herself comfortably with Mr. Moe, alias T. White.

Mrs. Jonquil looked at Mr. Jonquil, as though to say: "You're the story-teller in this family."

"INTERMISSION until tomorrow night," said Mr. Jonquil.

37

Mr. Jonquil's Fairy Tale

"ONCE upon a time," began Mr. Jonquil.

"Do they all begin that way?" asked Jane.

"Yes," said her father. "That's what makes it a fairy tale, because once upon a time is fairy time."

"Very well," said Jane. "Begin."

"Once upon a time," began Mr. Jonquil a second time, "there was a king's son who was wandering all alone, far from his bell-hung horse cropping at the edge of the forest where the trees were mighty in darkness. He came to a clearing in the woods; and in the middle of the clearing he saw a house. Boldly he went to the door, for night was darkening the land, and he heard far off the shrill notes of bugles seeking him.

"He knocked once, and the door seemed to open by itself. Inside, it was not like a house at all, but like a castle. On a platform overhung with cloth of gold he saw a golden bed; and lying in the golden bed, asleep, was a beautiful lady."

"A princess," said Jane.

"Exactly," said Mr. Jonquil. "The king's son looked around, and he saw an old man with a beard that reached to

the floor. The king's son spoke to him, but got no answer. So he lay down beside the door to sleep, and had no fear."

"Then what happened?" asked Jane.

"I'll tell you," said her mother. "If your father continues to wax lyrical, we'll never get to the end."

"Very well," said Mr. Jonquil. "Now there's sure to be a marriage."

"Of course," said Mrs. Jonquil.

"Of course," echoed Jane.

Mr. Jonquil's Fairy Tale
(Concluded by Mrs. Jonquil)

"WHEN DAWN came," said Mrs. Jonquil, "the king's son awoke with a start. He brushed sleep from his eyes and stood up. And there, beside him, stood the beautiful lady. But the old man with the long beard had vanished.

"The princess, for that's what she was, smiled and held out her hand to the king's son.

" 'When I came yesterday,' the prince said, 'there was an old man here who is here no longer. Who might that have been?'

" 'That was a wizard,' the princess explained. 'He had to be here till you came.'

" 'He knew I was coming?' asked the prince in amazement.

41

" 'Yes,' she replied. 'You see, he thought it all up. That was to make peace between your father and mine.'

" 'He was very thoughtful,' said the king's son.

"As he spoke, the house and all that was in it vanished away. They stood in the open. Far off they heard bugles, and then they saw the flash of flags—her father's and his.

"Then they were married. And you know what," concluded Mrs. Jonquil.

"They lived happily after," said Jane.

"Oh, indubitably," said Mr. Jonquil.

The Life and Happy Times
of Mrs. Jonquil (Concluded)

"MORE LIFE, more happy times," said Jane.

"REEL TWO," said Mr. Jonquil.

"I had a billy goat cart," said Mrs. Jonquil. "The billy goat had whiskers and horns. The cart was red, with green wheels. When friends came, we played getting married, and after the ceremony the cart was the bridal carriage in which the bride and bridegroom rode away on their honeymoon.

"Sometimes," Mrs. Jonquil went on, "I was the preacher and performed the marriage ceremony, even though I was a girl; but it couldn't be helped, because we didn't always have a boy around."

"A girl who could be a knight could be a preacher," said Mr. Jonquil.

"I liked being the preacher," said Mrs. Jonquil. "But I

43

also wanted to be the bridegroom, the bride's father, the best man, the bride, the bridesmaid, and the maid of honor."

"Tell about riding away after the ceremony," said Jane.

"There was just barely room for two in the billy goat cart," said Mrs. Jonquil, "and they had to sit on the floor. Sometimes the only way you could tell the bride from the bridegroom was by the lace curtain she was wrapped in, with a taffeta sash from a party dress around the middle. You see, we played getting married even when there were no boys around, so often the bridegroom was a girl, too."

"CLOSE-UP," said Mr. Jonquil. " 'Do you take this man'—

who was really a woman—'to be your lawful wedded husband?' 'I do,' said the bride. 'Do you take this woman to be your lawful wedded wife?' 'I do,' said the bridegroom, smoothing down her dress."

"Exactly," said Mrs. Jonquil.

"What about the billy goat?" asked Jane.

"Once a goat, always a goat," said Mr. Jonquil. "You could depend on him not to get married under false pretenses."

"He was very patient," said Mrs. Jonquil.

"Next scene," said Jane.

"A barn," said Mrs. Jonquil. "In the foreground, a stack of hay. CLOSE-UP: Miss Pomfret on the roof."

Mr. Jonquil: "She jumps!"

Jane: "She lands in the hay!"

"Oh, it used to seem so far down to the haystack," said Mrs. Jonquil. "But when I saw it again a few years ago, it wasn't so far down, and the roof of the barn wasn't so high."

"Why not?" asked Jane.

"Because the roof and the haystack were still the same size," said Mrs. Jonquil, "but I had grown up."

THE END